PEAK PERIL

A HIGH-RISE MYSTERY

SHARNA JACKSON

Published by Knights Of

Knights Of Ltd, Registered Offices:
119 Marylebone Road, London, NW1 5PU

www.knightsof.media

First published 2022
001

First published in the UK by Knights Of, 2021

Set in Baskerville
Design by Marssaié Jordan
Typeset by Marssaié Jordan
Printed and bound in the UK

A CIP catalogue record for this book will be available from the British Library

ISBN: PB: 9781913311254
2 4 6 8 10 9 7 5 3 1

I celebrated World Book Day 2022 with this gift from my local bookseller and Knights Of

WORLD BOOK DAY

World Book Day's mission is to offer every child and young person the opportunity to read and love books by giving you the chance to have a book of your own.

To find out more, and for fun activities including our monthly book club, video stories and book recommendations visit worldbookday.com

World Book Day is a charity funded by publishers and booksellers in the UK and Ireland.

World Book Day is also made possible by generous sponsorship from National Book Tokens and support from authors and illustrators.

1

When Pap said leaving the city for a long weekend would be good for us, I 100% agreed.

I stared out of the minibus window, content and comfortable. Outside, shades of green and blue striped by. Inside, I covered my ears, blocking out a backseat conversation about the beauty of some actor. I didn't recognise their name, or care about their shade of lipstick.

It was time to care about us. A break in the country, away from The Tri – the estate where we lived – was something my sister and I needed.

Respite from crime was required – there had been two murders there, in the last year alone.

Two murders too many, but both swiftly solved by Norva and me.

We were excellent investigators now, but we needed a second to step away to sit back. To put death aside, for a moment. To be normal again.

My sister wasn't so sure. Norva scratched her neck and shook her head. 'Nik,' she said, nudging me in the ribs. 'That sign just said *Sheffield*, didn't it? Where's that, then? Is it in like Zone Six, or what?'

I rolled my eyes at her reflection. She saw me and stuck out her tongue in response. 'Sheffield's not in London,' I said. 'It's at least 140 miles away.' I looked at her. 'You're supposed to be smart.'

'Yeah,' said Norva. 'I know, I know – and shush, I *am* smart. I'm well clever. I just don't want to believe it, I guess.' She leaned over me to look out of the window. 'Where are all the *people*? Where are the *shops*?'

'We have everything we need. What do you want to buy?'

Norva shrugged. 'I don't know. Something? Anything? We have that fifty quid saved from October–'

Given to us by a dead woman. I shuddered at the memory.

'–where we going to spend it? There's nothing here but sheep. Imagine if we brought one of those woolly friends home? Pap would be like –'

She slapped her hands against her face and

made a shocked expression. I smiled. 'Pap wouldn't be pleased; no. Ringo might be though.'

Ringo. Our Jack Russell. Hates to nuzzle, loves to tussle.

'Yeah, he'd be galloping all over these hills,' said Norva. '*I* won't be though,' she said, slumping in her seat and crossing her arms.

'But *that's* exactly why you're here, Miss Alexander!' said Ms Chan. 32ish. P.E. Teacher. Countryside preacher. She turned in her seat to look back at us. 'This is what Girls Get Going! is for. Encouraging young ladies from busy cities and towns, like you, to slow down for a moment; to explore and appreciate the great outdoors. And there's no better outdoors than the Peak District, believe me. Enjoy breathing in some fresh, clean air for once.'

Norva kissed her teeth. 'I don't know about this fresh air you speak of, Miss, because the further away from London we get, the itchier I feel. Something ain't right up here.'

Ms Chan looked at me and rolled her eyes. I stifled a slight laugh.

'It ain't funny, Nik. It's also *well* sexist. Why can't boys come too, Miss? That ain't right. If George was here, it would be much better.'

George Shah. 14. Norva's friend. 'Besties to the end' is how he describes them.

I couldn't say I was missing him.

The minibus screeched and took a sharp left. We gripped the headrests in front of us.

'*Now* it's getting interesting,' said Norva, grinning.

The wheels of the bus crunched over grey gravel.

'Nearly there, girls!' shouted a smiling Ms Chan.

2

'Welcome to Sheaf Hill Hall, your home for the weekend!' Ms Chan shouted, pulling bags from the bus, placing them on the long driveway.

'Okay, alright now,' Norva said, impressed. 'The old-timey elegance this house is serving, the faded glamour jumps out. Vintage vibes.' Norva reached into her jacket pocket for her phone. She leaned back to take in the full view of the surely once grand, now certainly crumbling, stately home. She took a photograph. 'Who lives here, then? You reckon they'll take fifty pounds for it?'

Ms Chan laughed. 'No. Not a chance.'

'Sad,' Norva replied. She leaned over me, putting her phone into my face. 'Look – no filter needed, just a banging pic.'

'It is a good photograph, yes,' I replied.

'I'm sending it to George,' she said, returning to her phone. 'Show him what he's missing.'

She jabbed at the screen, then raised it in the air. Norva sighed. She folded at the waist. 'Ms Chan!' she wailed. 'What's going on? I've got like one bar of signal.'

'That's good!' Ms Chan replied.

'How so?' Norva asked, rubbing her forehead. 'Don't give me noise about appreciating the moment, now.'

'Norva, the point is to get away. To not stare down at your phone, but to look up at the world instead.'

'Pfft, please. That doesn't work for me – and neither does this phone now. It's useless.' Norva pushed it back into her pocket.

'It's not,' I said. 'It can make notes and keep photos.' I shrugged. 'It might be useful.'

Norva looked at me, her eyes shone. 'Oh, might it now? You thinking of doing a bit of investigating, are you? A little light snooping? A sprinkle of scammery?' She rubbed her hands together.

'No, no. I was just saying –'

'– well, keep talking Nik, because you know I'm up for that. Always.'

I shook my head. 'We're on a break, Norva.'

'Never!' She hissed.

'Grab your bags, girls!' said Ms Chan. 'Deborah!' she shouted to a woman waiting with outstretched arms by the entrance of the hall.

'Ey up, Cinds!' Deborah shouted back. She was tall, with a Yorkshire drawl. She embraced Ms Chan, while Norva, the other girls and I gathered around. 'Everyone, meet Ms Cocker,' said Ms Chan. 'She's in charge of all of this.' Ms Chan beamed at Ms Cocker.

'And she's your friend?' said Norva.

Ms Cocker nodded. 'We've been friends for *years.*'

'A very long time,' said Ms Chan. 'Since Hallam.'

'Hallam?' I asked. 'What's that?'

'Sheffield Hallam University,' said Ms Cocker. She looked at Ms Chan, grinned, squealed, then rubbed her arms. 'Oh, I'm *so* glad you're here!'

While they reconnected, I looked up and around Sheaf Hill Hall. My eyes were drawn to the window, to our right. There was a silver car with a soft roof beneath it and a tall, thin man stood in the frame. He held up yellowing net curtains with one hand and had a landline phone in the other. I couldn't hear what he was saying, but I knew it wasn't positive, judging by his face. I nudged Norva.

'What's his beef?' she whispered. The man spoke rapidly down the phone. He tutted, shook his head at the bus, then towards our group. When he saw us, he narrowed his eyes and quickly dropped the curtain.

3

'Ignore that one,' laughed a light voice behind us. 'He's reyt mardy.'

'Reyt? Mardy?' whispered Norva. 'What language is that, then?'

'I think it means he's very moody,' I said.

'In Yorkshian?' asked Norva.

'Yep,' laughed the woman. We turned to look at her. Body small, hair curly, teeth pearly white. 'That's what it means. And really, pay him no mind,' she said, with a wave of the hand. 'Tom's always like that. Tom Thorne by name, thorn by nature. He owns the hall.' The woman rolled her eyes.

'*For now*,' said Norva. 'I'm gonna make him an offer.'

The woman laughed. She placed her clipboard under her arm and put out her hand. 'Good luck with that. I'm Millie, by the way. Millie Greenwood.' We shook her hand and introduced ourselves.

'Nice to meet you,' I said.

Millie nodded and smiled. 'I work with Debs on Girls Get Going! I'm her assistant –'

'My everything, you mean!' said Ms Cocker, interrupting, shouting over our conversation. Millie grinned at her.

'And since we're doing intros, him over there,' she pointed to a man trimming a bush with shears at the end of the drive. 'That's Jake. Now he's *great*,' she said.

Norva looked at me and wriggled her eyebrows. Millie noticed and shook her head. 'No, no – nothing like that!' She looked down at her clipboard and coughed. 'Anika and Norva Alexander, hmmm?'

'I prefer Nik, but yes,' I said. She nodded and edited my name on her paper. 'Alright, well, let me show you to your room. We have a special spot for you.'

'Loving that,' said Norva, rubbing her hands together. 'We *are* special, so thanks for recognising that.'

'Then follow me,' said Millie.

I put my backpack on and Norva slung her bag over her shoulder. I looked over at the rolling green hills, before walking behind Millie.

Sheaf Hill Hall's ceilings were tall. Red paint,

once on the wall, had flaked off. It now lay in messy, random clumps on the floor. Tom Thorne's heavy wood door was closed, but we could hear him muttering on the other side. Millie hurried us along, before we could make out any specific words. Opposite his office, was a large map of the huge house, and the vast grounds it stood on.

'This is what we call '*The Gathering*,' said Millie, pointing into a large, dark wooden panelled dining hall. 'We'll all meet in there later.'

We poked our heads in to look. Norva nodded her appreciation. 'Yep,' she said. 'Good. This will be our living room.'

Millie walked us around the corner and into a small corridor with five closed doors.

'And here we are,' said Millie, triumphantly.

'The ground floor?' Norva asked. She pursed her lips and looked at me.

'Yep, next to us and Ms Chan.'

'Next to the adults?' Norva sighed, slapping her arms against her sides. 'This feels like punishment to me.'

Millie opened the door to our room. 'These rooms down here are *the best*, I promise. You're lucky.' She looked at us, loitering by the doorway.

'What you waiting for? Go on, go in! Make yourselves at home.' We stepped in, placing out bags on the floor. 'Get settled and enjoy!' Millie said. 'When you hear the bell go, join us in The Gathering.'

4

Norva looked around the room, her hands on her hips. 'We've been done dirty here,' she said.

'How?' I asked. 'What do you mean?'

'What I *mean* is,' she said, closing the door slightly. 'That Millie sold this room to us like it was something special. Ain't nothing special about it.'

The room was fine. It was small, clean, mostly white. Bunk beds were pushed against the wall. Norva threw her bag on the top one. 'I'm not even calling dibs; you know it's mine.' She climbed up the short ladder, lay on her back and looked up at the ceiling.

I wasn't going to argue with her. I don't like heights, even though we live on the top floor of a tower block. That's probably the reason. I placed my bag on the floor and sat on my bed. I looked out of the window and understood why Millie said this room was special. The view was incredible, very different from home. There I look over our estate, over London. Here there was grass and trees as far as my eyes could see. A bunch of picked wildflowers stood on the windowsill, their vase was wrapped in a yellow ribbon. I moved them aside and opened the window. I leaned out and breathed in.

I closed my eyes, appreciating nature, enjoying the silence.

'Traitor,' Norva said, looking down at me from her bunk. 'Look at you, thinking about leaving the city, swapping it for country life.'

'What are you talking about? *You're* the one who wants to buy the Hall.'

Norva laughed and rolled over. 'Yeah, I suppose. Ooh, I'll only really consider it *if* there's a bathroom in here. I'm not up for sharing with randoms.' She shuddered. 'Beyond gross.'

I pointed to a closed door, at the end of the room, opposite the bunks. 'Maybe in there?'

'Check then, please?' she begged. 'It's too far for me to walk.'

I sighed and walked to the door. Behind it, was a tiny bathroom. A toilet, a small sink and narrow shower stall. 'Look,' I said. 'There's your bathroom.'

'Great,' she said. 'We're back in business then. I'll talk to that Tom Thorne when we see him.'

'You do that,' I said, opening my bag and unpacking my three blue t-shirts.

'Wait. Shush!' Norva hissed. She leaned over her bed, her braids hanging upside down. 'What's that?'

'I'm not making any noise,' I whispered, raising my hands.

'It's like scratching, like little rats running around.'

I stood in silence for a moment, then I could hear it too. It was coming from the corridor. Norva put a finger to her lips, then jabbed it towards the door. She nodded and raised her eyebrows.

She was asking me to investigate. And so it began.

Again.

I walked slowly to the door, holding my breath. There, two faces peered into our room through the gap. I looked up at Norva and nodded. She sprang off the top bunk, landed on her feet on the floor and pulled the door open.

5

'Who are you? What do you want?' Norva demanded, her left eyebrow raised. 'Why are you spying on us, huh?'

The two girls behind the door gasped, stepped backwards, and held on to each other. The slightly shorter one held onto a book in her hands and stared at me, fear evident in her eyes.

'Norva...' I started.

'Don't *Norva* me!' she shouted. 'Well? Speak!'

The taller one, with bob length braids stood forward. 'No need to lose your voice about it. I'm Tasha and, like, sorry to scare you but we –'

'Defo didn't mean to,' said the smaller girl. 'I'm Sophie.' She looked up at Norva from under her heavy blonde fringe and put her hand out for us to shake. Norva eyed it suspiciously.

'We were just looking around –' Tasha said.

'You know, trying to make friends, figuring this building out – seeing who has the best room,'

Sophie laughed. 'Working out how *we* ended up on the ground floor.'

'Right?' said Norva, relaxing slightly. 'I was thinking the same thing. I'm Norva, this is my sister, Nik.'

'Ooh, *sisters*?' said Sophie. 'That's cool.'

'Sometimes,' I said.

Tasha nodded. 'I know *that* feeling. I have a little brother; he's just turned three. That kid is a lot, so I'm glad to be away. I'm looking forward to some decent sleep for once.'

'I ain't planning on doing much sleeping, to be honest,' said Sophie. She shook her notebook at us. 'I'm gonna use the time and space to think, to sketch and to write. It's well beautiful here, innit? Inspiring.'

I nodded. 'It's very different from home.'

'Where's home for you, then?' asked Tasha. 'We're from Harlow.'

Norva turned to me. 'Where's that? Zone Six?'

I shook my head. 'No, but it's much closer to us than Sheffield.'

Sophie laughed. 'You from London, then? I am too, originally. I was born there, in Barking, right by the Creek.'

'Hmmm. We've been there once,' said Norva. 'It's all right. It's no South East, though. The best ends in the city, no cap.'

Sophie smiled. 'If you say so.' She leaned into our room, then looked back at Tasha. 'They *definitely* have the better room, Tash. *Much* better view.' Sophie looked at me. 'Wanna swap?'

Norva and I shook our heads simultaneously.

'How many rooms have you seen?' I asked. 'When did you get here?'

'Early,' said Tasha. 'Way too early.'

Sophie nodded. 'Our teacher, Mrs Marsh, she wanted to get on the first train. She's a true eager beaver. As for your first question, yours is the fourth room we've seen – you two win the battle of the bunks.'

'We also went into that office near the entrance, with the owner, didn't we?' said Tasha.

'Yeah, that was properly tense,' said Sophie, shuddering.

Norva stood tall. 'Oh yeah? How so?'

'Well,' said Tasha. 'That Ms Cocker took us in to meet him –'

'– and he was mad frosty,' added Sophie. 'Dishing out dirty looks.'

'After we left his office, and she stayed behind,

we heard him go “this is the last time”,’ said Tasha.

‘But, he like, growled it,’ said Sophie.

Norva’s eyes lit up. ‘Interesting,’ she said.

A bell rang through Sheaf Hill Hall.

‘It must be time to go to The Gathering,’ I said.

‘I reckon,’ said Tasha. ‘Well, it was good to meet you. Maybe see you later?’

‘Maybe,’ said Norva. She smiled at me and rubbed her hands together.

6

I shuffled on the long, uncomfortable wooden bench and looked around The Gathering. On my first, quick count, there were at least a hundred girls here, from across the country. Norva inched closer to me. I was in the middle of a row, between her and Ms Chan; the worst place to be. Trapped and unable to leave without making everyone else stand up. I sighed.

Norva looked over and patted my back. 'Don't worry it will be over soon, and you'll get some space,' she whispered. 'Look – they're about to start chatting.'

Ms Deborah Cocker, Millie Greenwood, and the tall man, Tom Thorne, stepped up on a raised platform in front of us, their audience. Ms Cocker clapped her hands together twice, and the hall quickly fell silent.

'Impressive crowd control,' said Norva.

'Girls, your attention for a moment.' said

Ms Cocker. A hundred faces turned to hers. She smiled. 'Welcome to Sheaf Hill Hall, for the fifth annual Girls Get Going! gathering.' She punched the air awkwardly, and beside her Millie clapped, beaming up at her.

Norva stifled a laugh. 'Mess,' she said, under her breath.

The girls around us clapped, and we joined in – after being nudged by Ms Chan.

'I know, for some of you, you're taking your first, big, green leaps into the unknown,' said Ms Cocker. 'I'm proud and pleased you are trusting us to let us guide your way –'

'Oh my days,' whispered Norva, throwing her head back. 'It's not like we're going to the moon, we're going on the moors. Calm it down.'

'I can't wait to personally meet all of you,' Ms Cocker beamed, waving her hand across the audience. 'And to reconnect with old friends.' She pointed to Ms Chan, who clutched her chest and smiled in return. Tom Thorne, watching their interaction, shifted his weight and rolled his eyes.

'This weekend is going to be *packed* with activities – we're going to walk, and talk of course, but we'll do some much more: orienteering, climbing –'

I shut my eyes, hoping she wouldn't mention abseiling. The last time we were involved with that, it ended in murder.

'–rock climbing, abseiling…'

Oh no.

'Wait, wait, wait,' said Tom Thorne, talking over Ms Cocker. Millie looked up at him and scowled. 'This is all very nice, but a bit boring – don't you think, girls?'

Ms Cocker turned her head towards him, her white cheeks flushed red. 'Well,' she flustered. '*I* don't think so, Millie and I have a packed programme –'

'Do you want some *real* adventure?' he said, rubbing his chin. 'Eh?'

An electrified murmur rippled through the now-excited crowd. 'I do!' Norva shouted, thrusting her arm in the air. 'I can't be bothered to climb.'

Ms Chan leaned over me. 'Norva, stop,' she said through gritted teeth. 'Put your hand down!'

Tom smiled. 'Let me tell you a story. Sheaf Hill Hall is mine now, but it used to belong to Daddy –'

Norva snorted. 'This grown man calls his Pap *Daddy* you know.'

'That was, until he died. Two months ago.'

The gathered girls gasped. Millie and Ms Cocker shared a look and shook their heads.

Ms Cocker grabbed Tom's arm. 'Not now, Tom. OK?' she said through a gritted-toothed smile.

Tom put his hands up. 'It's OK, Deborah, it's alright. He was old, it was his time to go. When he *was* alive though, he always told me about the Sheaf Stash – treasure that's buried somewhere here in the Peaks around the Hall.'

Norva sat up straight. 'Keep going, Tom, say more,' she whispered. I looked over the girls in the hall and spotted Tasha and Sophie nudging each other at another table. Sophie's notebook was open in front of her and she scribbled furiously.

'That's what Daddy used to say, anyway. So, I want you to find it.'

'Deal!' Norva shouted.

Ms Cocker stepped in front of Tom and pulled his arm. 'Now then, Tom,' she said, her words gentle, her eyes anything but. 'We don't want to do that do we?'

'I do!' Sophie shouted from a faraway table. 'I defo want that!'

Millie closed her eyes and shook her head. She gripped her clipboard with both hands.

'It will be fun, and you just might get rich!' laughed Tom. 'Who doesn't want to be rich? Look at the giant map near the entrance for clues,' he shouted, stepping off the stage. 'That's where Daddy said they were, anyway. And if you find it, well, give me a cut!' He reached up to pat a furious, tight-faced Millie on her arm, and then he walked through the hall, head high, his suit jacket swishing behind him.

7

A door at the end of The Gathering burst open and hit the wall. A good 47% of us jumped. A line of servers walked out, carrying steaming trays of food.

'Aw, yes!' said Norva. 'I'm well hungry.'

Ms Cocker, confused by the impending dinner but welcoming the distraction, raised her arms and shouted, 'Tea is served!' She turned to Millie, whispered something with wide eyes, then, together, they stepped off stage.

An arm poked itself between Norva and I, placing a napkin-wrapped set of steel cutlery between us and a bottle of something called Henderson's Relish on the table. Norva opened the bottle and sniffed.

'What's this, then?' she asked.

'The best,' said Ms Chan, with a smile. 'Just you wait.'

Dinner was a giant Yorkshire pudding, the

biggest I'd ever seen, and it was filled with sausage, mashed potatoes, peas and chunky onion gravy. Norva finished hers before I was even a third of the way through mine. Dessert was a traditional (apparently) Yorkshire curd tart.

'This is *elite*,' said Norva, swallowing heaped spoonfuls at a time. I pushed mine towards her. 'You don't like the texture, do you?' she asked. I nodded. 'Sucks for you,' she said, shrugging and scrapping my portion onto her plate.

After dinner, we sat on the grass with Ms Chan and the rest of our group from school. I held my phone in my hand, ready to turn on the torch. It was about to get dark.

'And then,' Ms Chan said with a low voice. 'Our hero turned to face the voices, those of the crying children…' she paused and looked around at us. 'But there was nobody, not a soul there.' She put the torch under her chin and bulged her eyes. 'Nothing but two sets of tiny wet footprints on the footbridge, leading to the river.'

The girls shuddered, but not Norva. 'Weak,' she said, flatly. 'And not scary.'

My stomach rumbled loudly and *everyone* heard. 'Now *that's* frightening!' Norva laughed.

I shook my head at my sister. 'Ms Chan?' I asked. 'I'm not feeling great after trying that tart. I need to... use the bathroom.'

Ms Chan nodded. 'Of course.'

'I'm going with her,' said Norva, getting to her feet. She pulled my arm to stand me up, and we walked back into Sheaf Hill Hall.

'I can't wait to live here – on the weekends only, though,' said Norva. 'I've decided we still need our place in the city.'

'Okay,' I said, holding my stomach. 'That makes sense.'

Norva looked around the entrance and headed to the map. She snatched my phone from my hand and took a picture. 'We're going to need this, because if *anyone's* getting hold of the Sheaf Stash, it's going to be us.'

'Can we talk about this later, Norva?' I said. 'I need –'

'Oh, they were *not* happy, Carla, not at all!' said Tom Thorne from behind his door. Norva cocked her head towards it and moved closer. I shook my head – I really needed to go – but she put her finger on my lip. She listened. I crossed my legs.

'Why me, Carls? Why? I *wish* I never said yes… yeah, yeah, I know, I know – but, but but, Daddy had loads of kids, so I'm told. So why is it my problem? I know – but I just don't want it. I want to go back to Leeds… yeah, I miss the brewery, but nowt I can do about that now.'

Norva rubbed her chin, then mimicked drinking from a pint glass.

'Sheaf Hill Hall's on its last legs, Carly. And all this charity work with poor girls –'

I sighed and shook my head. Norva narrowed her eyes.

'– is doing nothing. I have to do something *bold.* Alright, love, Yeah, yes. I'll be home soon.'

My stomach purred. 'Norva,' I mouthed. This time she nodded, and we ran down the corridor to our room. Once inside, I threw open the door to the bathroom, slammed it shut, making sure it was locked. Norva has no respect for privacy, so I had to make sure.

She stood at the other side door. 'Well, well, well!' she said excitedly. 'Look what we have here.'

'Norva, please don't talk, I'm busy –'

'A little cosy case, a simple way to take our sleuthing national!'

'Please, be quiet.'

'We find the Sheffield Stash, save the Hall, get fame and riches. You in?'

I stayed silent.

'I said are you in, sis?'

I sighed. 'Yes, Norva. I'm in.'

I heard her squeal and clap her hands with delight.

8

I washed my hands and opened the door. Norva was standing in the doorway, grinning.

'It's going to be so good, right?'

'Hmmm… I *was* hoping for a break,' I said.

'*Pfft*, she said, waving her hand. 'You can pause when you're old, or dead. Choose one, but for now, we keep it moving.' She jumped up and down on the spot. 'Let's get back to the group?'

I nodded. 'I want to hear more of Ms Chan's spooky stories.' I smiled at my sister.

'They're the worst, right?' Norva laughed.

We stepped out of our room, and straight into Millie, hugging her clipboard close to her chest. 'Oh, sorry love,' she said to Norva. 'You alright there?'

Norva nodded. 'Yeah, we're good.'

'I just came to see if you we're feeling better, Nik?' she asked. Ms Chan said you were poorly.'

'I'm fine,' I said, because I was now. 'Are *you* OK?' I asked. I took a sideways look at Norva. 'That was interesting, what happened with Tom Thorne.' I could see Norva smiling from the corner of my eye.

'Yeah!' said Norva. 'Is it true about the treasure, the Sheaf Stash?'

Millie shook her head. 'Nope, it's just a silly legend. None of us who grew up around here believe it. Tom's just… a troublemaker. Ignore him. Go join your group – there's not much better than scary stories at Sheaf Hill Hall in the dark. Off you pop, now.'

We smiled and ran down the corridor. I turned to look at Millie, who was watching us leave.

'And, that, my girls, is the legend of the big black dog of Bunting Nook,' said Ms Chan as Norva and I sat back down on the grass. 'If you see it, never, *ever* touch it. Don't approach. You're lucky though, it's not really interested in you.'

'Why not?' asked Norva. 'What's the deal with this dog, then?'

'Ahh,' said Ms Chan. 'It looks for car drivers – then, it snares only the male passengers.' Ms Chan howled like a wolf, and then laughed.

Norva shook her head and sighed. 'Embarrassing,' she said. She lay back on the grass as Ms. Chan told another tale. Norva began to sing under her breath. 'When I am a rich girl, I'll have Sheaf Hill Hall, and all the money, no need to bawl.'

'That's not your best work,' I whispered. She looked up at me, her laughing eyes, shining in the dark.

'Brilliant, just brilliant!' said Tom Thorne. He'd left his office, and was now leaning by his car, having a seemingly friendly animated conversation with a slightly younger man.

'Who's Tom chatting to?' asked Norva, turning over and leaning on her elbows.

I squinted. 'I think that's Jake. The gardener.'

'Millie's man?' said Norva.

'She said he wasn't.'

'With her mouth, yeah, but her eyes told me something different,' said Norva.

'Absolutely fantastic,' said Tom, looking at Jake. 'You just might have fixed that for me.'

He reached over and slapped Jake on the back. Two hard taps. He pointed at him with his car keys. 'I'll owe you one if that works,' he said, before getting into his car, and speeding away with a screech across the gravel.

'OK, girls,' said Ms Chan, she clapped her hands. 'It's just gone nine, time to retire.'

9

My stomach turned over loudly, waking me up. I reached under my pillow for my phone. 12:30. I was hungry, and breakfast wasn't for another eight hours. I lay back down and shut my eyes. I needed to go back to sleep. Hunger couldn't find me there.

'Should have eaten more dinner,' Norva muttered from the bunk above. 'Then your roaring belly wouldn't be waking me up like this.'

'Sorry,' I said.

'Nah, don't apologise, it's good.'

'It is?'

'Yeah,' she said, leaning over. 'It means we can go searching for snacks. Maybe some spare sausages, or something.'

'Searching for snacks, or searching for trouble?' I asked.

Norva leaned down to look at me. 'Why not both?'

My stomach groaned in response.

'See, your belly gets it,' she said. She climbed down the short ladder to the floor. 'Let's go.'

We slowly opened our door and peered out. The door diagonal to ours was ajar. Light from the room spilled out into the corridor and so did sounds. We could hear music, quiet laughing, wine being poured into glasses, then those glasses clinking.

I looked at Norva and stepped into the corridor for a closer look and listen. Norva stood behind me.

'Ah, I'm reyt glad you're here.' That was Ms Cocker, definitely.

'It's so good to be back,' said Ms Chan. 'Can't believe we left it so long!'

'That's just how it goes when you grow up, doesn't it? Shame. We just get too busy.'

'We do. Well, this feels like being back in first year, this does.'

Ms Cocker laughed. 'It does, doesn't it? *Owl or blades, lass? Owl or blades?* Remember that?'

Norva wrinkled her nose, wondering what that meant.

Ms Chan burst out laughing. 'How can I

forget?' She sipped loudly at her drink. 'You've got a good thing here, you have – you're doing so well!'

'Well…' Ms Cocker protested.

'You are!' said Ms Chan. 'It's a great business. And I like that Millie! Very smart, official. Where did you find her? Watch out, though! I think she wants your job. Keen.'

Ms Cocker shushed Ms Chan. She giggled. 'She's *just* next door,' she whispered. 'Not that you'd hear her – she's quiet as a mouse, that one.'

'Hmmm,' said Ms Chan.

'Hmmm,' said Ms Cocker. 'She's local, Millie is. She was *so* eager to work here with me, wanted the job so much, no other candidate came close. Plus, I think she *really* needs the money.'

'Who doesn't?' said Ms Chan.

'Tom doesn't.'

'Ooh, tell me about him,' said Ms Chan. 'I like him… he seems dangerous.'

Dangerous didn't seem like a positive attribute to me. Norva put her hand to her mouth to stifle a laugh.

'He's… not bad,' said Ms Cocker. 'An interesting man, but he's always on the phone to his… wife, Cinds.' She sighed. 'He's not for you.

Don't get involved. Trust me.'

'Aww, shame,' said Ms Chan, the disappointment palpable in her voice.

'Honestly, it would be better if he just left,' said Ms Cocker. 'Left me alone.'

'Is it now?' Norva whispered, leaning forward to hear more. As she did, our door creaked loudly. The music in the other room stopped suddenly.

'Busted!' whispered Norva. She pulled on my shoulder, and we hurried back to our room and gently closed the door. My stomach groaned.

Norva laughed. 'Your stomach stays empty, but this story just gets fuller. It's poetic.'

'No, painful,' I said, standing in our moon-bathed room. I looked out of the window. 'It's so *quiet* here.'

'Yeah, it's weird,' said Norva, joining me. 'I can, like, hear my heart beating and blood pumping all the time. Don't like it. Wait – who's *that*? *What's* that? It ain't that big black dog is it?' She dug her nails into my arm.

It wasn't, at least I think it wasn't. A dark figure paced past our window. A cap on their head covered their eyes. My heart rate definitely increased by a few beats.

'You're not scared of Ms Chan's story, are you, Norva?'

'Nah, nah,' she released her grip on my arm. 'I just want to know who's pacing these Peaks in the middle of the night. Make it make sense.'

I put my face against the window. 'I think that's Jake,' I said, and as I did, he looked directly at me. He gasped when our eyes met, then he put his head down and walked quicker.

'What's he doing? At this time?'

'Maybe he's working?' said Norva, climbing up to her bunk. 'Maybe they roll differently, up here in the North? Time means nothing, maybe?'

I didn't believe that for one second. I got into bed and shut my eyes. My stomach grumbled. I covered my ears.

10

'I still can't believe I've only got one bar,' said Norva. 'How is it possible to have one-bar places, in this England?'

I rolled over and looked at my phone. 08:00. I could eat soon. 'What's the urgency?' I said, my voice croaking.

'Well, I want to chat with George, don't I, but it might be for the best, because I don't know what the time difference is between here and London.'

'There isn't one.'

'Don't believe you. Also, anyways, I was actually trying to get ahead with the case a bit.'

'There is no case, Norva.'

'Not yet, there isn't, but there will be,' she said. 'I can feel it in my bones – and my waters.' She lay back for a moment. 'All I was trying to do was Google Tom Thorne. That's it! Wasn't asking for much.' She fiddled with her phone a moment longer. 'Gah, useless,' she said. She threw her covers off and stepped down the ladder. 'I'm going in the shower; one good thing about being here is that we don't have to wear uniform.' She stopped by the door and crouched down. She rubbed her chin, and chuckled.

'What?' I asked, sitting up.

'What did you just say about there being no case? Looks like you spoke too soon. Check this out!'

She sat on my bed, next to me and handed me a note. It was handwritten, small capital letters on thin white card, with a small fold at the top. I stared at the words.

If you want to get ahead, follow the yellow ribbons instead. Seek the first one, fifty steps North of the red.

'Hmmm,' I said.

'Hmmm?' said Norva. 'That's it? Come on, a case has commenced! Who put this under our door, when and why?'

'OK,' I said, rubbing my eyes. 'Let's work backwards.'

'If you wish,' said Norva.

'Well, someone wants us to follow another path today, during whatever activity it is we're doing.'

'The Sheaf Stash!' Norva whispered, rubbing her hands together. 'This is the first clue, definitely!'

'Maybe. As for when… it had to have been between 12:45 and 08:00 this morning. I didn't see it before we listened in on Ms Chan and Ms Cockers conversation, did you?'

She shook her head. 'So, who do you think put it there?'

I shrugged. 'It could have been Ms Cocker and Ms Chan –'

'Why though? They wouldn't want us going off beat, would they? Who else?'

'Tom Thorne. He's the one who told us about the Sheaf Stash in the first place –'

'Yeah, but we saw him leave at like nine,' said Norva. 'Ooh, he could have got that Jake to put it here. They were having a good old friendly chat and he was creeping around in the middle of the night. We both saw him.'

'We did. He's a strong suspect. What about Millie?'

'She was asleep, that's what Cocker and Chan said.'

'But we don't have any evidence to prove that was the case, do we?' I replied.

Norva shook my shoulder. 'Yes, evidence!

Welcome back, detective, lovely to see you again.'

I ignored her. 'I don't know who yet.'

'But we're going to find out, aren't we? Aren't we?'

I nodded.

'Love to hear it.' Norva stood up and opened our door. 'There might be more evidence out here,' she said.

I leaned out to look. The door directly opposite ours, belonged to Tasha and Sophie, the girls we met yesterday. Their door was open, too and they were already dressed. When they saw us, Sophie gasped, and Tasha shut their door quickly.

'That girl, Sophie,' I said. 'She said she was a writer, didn't she?'

'Yeah,' said Norva, copying her. 'I'm gonna use the time and space to think, to sketch and to write.'

'Maybe she wrote this? Maybe it's a game?' I took a photo of it with my phone.

'Yes!' said Norva. 'To distract us while they find the Sheaf Stash and snatch the money and glory away from us.' Norva leaned on the door. 'Well, haha on you, Harlows – that's not going to happen!' she shouted at it.

'That's not helping,' I said.

She shrugged. 'I liked it, though.' She ran towards the bathroom. 'Either way, what will definitely help, what we're definitely going to do is follow this clue, rather than follow any Chan plan.'

'Norva, I don't know…'

'What's the worst that could happen?'

I narrowed my eyes.

'Yeah, don't answer that,' she laughed.

11

Outside The Gathering, Norva pulled on my arm. 'I know you're starving; I get it – but let's have a quick look at that map, just one more time?'

'We don't need to; we have a photo of it.'

'I know, but we might see something else in it, in real life.'

'Fine, OK,' I said. We walked over to it and peered at it. 'I'm not sure what I'm looking for.'

'Hopefully a big, red X, and we can take it from there,' said Norva her face close to the glass.

'It won't be that simple.'

'It might be.'

A voice laughed behind us. We turned to see Tom, in his office on the phone. Both feet were on his desk.

'It was good, wasn't it?' he laughed to the person on the other end. He saw us staring and gave us a small wave.

'He's changed,' said Norva leaning towards me.

'Maybe he thinks we're going to make him rich? Richer?' I said.

'Exactly?' she replied. 'Must be the reason.' She looked at the map again. 'I'm getting nothing from this,' she lowered her voice. 'But I got a lot from him,' She pointed her thumb at Tom's office. 'Let's eat!'

We joined the queue for the breakfast buffet. I peered past the glass. They had everything. Sausages, bacon, eggs, cereal. Toast was enough for me today. With some jam.

'I'm having one of everything,' said Norva, wrenching the tongs from my hand and piling her plate. 'You're just having that?' she said looking into mine. 'Thought you were hungry?'

'It will do,' I said.

'Suit yourself but know this – nothing tastes better than free food.'

Sophie laughed behind us. 'Innit though!' she said. Norva looked at me and narrowed her eyes, but quickly looked round at Sophie and smiled. Tasha stood behind her.

'Morning,' I said. 'Did you sleep well?'

'Too well,' said Tasha quietly. 'Do you think someone can sleep too much?'

'Doubt it,' said Norva.

'It's well weird, having that much deep, uninterrupted sleep,' she continued. 'I ain't used to it.' She shook her head.

'Well, I didn't sleep that much,' said Sophie, brightly. 'I stayed up, did some writing–'

'I bet you did,' Norva muttered.

'– I wrote by torch light. It was very cool, very proper, very romantic. I loved it,' she sighed.

'What were you writing?' I asked.

'Oh…' she said. 'Just a poem, for a… friend back home.'

Tasha stifled a laugh.

'What?' asked Norva.

'Nothing,' said Tasha. 'Sophie's just doing a Sophie – she's obsessed with this fool, Paul Stanley, she thinks she's got a chance and –'

Sophie nudged Tasha squarely in the ribs. 'Leave me! I just think he's nice, yeah?'

I needed to bring this investigation back to the facts. 'I see. So, did anything else interesting happen last night?'

Sophie looked up at Tasha, then they both shook their heads. 'Nope, nothing,' said Sophie.

She looked down at her breakfast. 'Well, this is getting cold. See you later, yeah?'

'You just might,' said Norva quietly. As they walked away, she leaned towards me. 'The Harlows are well sus. I can't trust them as far as I can throw them.'

I nodded. I wasn't 100% sure of them either.

As we sat down, Ms Cocker stood up. She clapped her hands twice.

'Here we go again,' said Norva.

'Good to see so many fresh faces this morning,' she grinned. 'To kick off our first full day, we're going to be doing a little orienteering activity on the grounds. Make sure you dress for any weather and wear sensible shoes. We'll meet outside in our school groups at 09:30.'

'Let the games begin!' said Millie, by Ms Cocker's side. She spotted me and waved. She rubbed her stomach and put her thumbs up. I nodded.

I was much better, thank you, Millie. I was ready for the day, whatever it brought.

12

Norva eyed Ms Cocker. She leaned towards me. 'I think we're underdressed, you know?' I looked at our outfits. We wore thin raincoats – mine blue, Norva's yellow – and our regular trainers on our feet. I glanced at Ms Cocker. She wore a North Face jacket – I only knew this from the logo stitched on it. Jeans tucked into thick socks, which were inside walking boots, already caked with dried mud. She wore mirrored sunglasses over her eyes. I could see myself staring at her in them.

'Right, girls,' she said. 'This is an easy, short and mostly flat route to get us used to the fine sport of orienteering. We're going to go in twos.'

Norva immediately grabbed my arm, as if I would choose to go with someone else. Ms Chan walked around our group, handing out small packages to each pair.

'Inside your sets are four things,' said Ms

Cocker, holding up as many fingers. 'A map, a compass, a piece of card and a pen.'

Norva opened our package and held the compass to the light. 'We're going to get so lost, like, how does this even work?'

'It's easy, you'll see,' said Ms Chan. 'Just listen.'

'You have one hour,' said Ms Cocker. 'This team,' she pointed at Norva and me. 'You will follow the red flags. You will see them on the map, and in real life. When you do spot one, go up to them, they won't bite,' she smiled. 'There will be a word written under the flag. Use your pen and piece of card to write it down and make a note, then move on to the next one. Within the hour, you should have a complete sentence or a short phrase.'

'Easy,' said Ms Chan.

'For you,' Norva replied. 'But it does actually sound quite fun.'

'It does,' I said. 'It's a blend of maths, science, geography and literature. I like it.'

'Told you,' said Ms Chan, beaming. 'I knew you'd like it!'

I opened the map and found the closest red flag on it. I looked up the hill in front of me, sure I could see it in the distance.

'There you go, you've got the hang of it already,' Ms Chan said. 'Go quickly! Look, the other schools are already on their way.' She lowered her voice. 'It's not a competition, but I totally want us to win.'

We looked up to see Tasha and Sophie holding their map between them. They stared at it intently, then walked up a hill to our right, disappearing into the woods. We glanced back at the Hall. Tom Thorne was outside, now. He held Ms Cockers elbow and was talking closely in her ear. They both looked up at us, and when we caught their eye, they quickly turned away.

13

'I thought she said this path was mostly flat,' Norva moaned as we walked up the hill. 'Lies. Actual lies.'

'It's not that bad,' I said. 'It's no worse than walking the stairs at home when the lifts are broken.'

'True,' she replied. 'How much further?'

I pointed at the flag, about fifty meters in front of us. 'It's just there.'

'Alright, not so far. I can do this.' I knew she could.

We approached the flag. Attached to it was a laminated piece of paper. The word 'owl' was typed on it.

I pulled the piece of card from the package. There were spaces for seven words. There was a comma between the third and fourth words and a question mark between the fourth and the fifth. I used the pen to write 'owl' in the first space. I peered at the paper.

'Owl…' I said, tucking the card under my chin and unfurling the map. 'Let's find the next flag, and figure this out,' I said, invested in my task.

Norva slapped the map out of my hands and fell to the floor. I put my foot out to stop it blowing away. 'Have you forgotten our mission already?' she said with a shake of her head. 'If you want to get ahead, follow the yellow ribbons instead. Seek the first one, fifty steps North of the red!'

'You remembered that word for word?'

'It's catchy, couldn't help it. Let's go do that now, instead of this.'

'But what about the phrase?'

'What about it?'

'I'd like to finish it, for completeness,' I said.

Norva sighed and pulled the card from under my chin. She looked at it while she stroked her upper lip, her weight on one foot. She suddenly stood up straight and flicked the paper. 'I know what this is!' she said. 'Good job we were sneaky this morning, or else we'd actually have to do this whole thing.'

'It was?'

'Yeah,' she said. 'Remember that weird thing Ms Cocker said to Channy last night?'

I thought for a moment. 'Oh yes, something about owls and… blades.'

'Exactly,' said Norva. 'Owls or Blades, lass? Owls or Blades. That totally fits. Still don't have a clue what it means, but it works for me.'

It worked for me, too. I wrote it onto the card and slipped it into my pocket.

'Look at us, NSquared, smashing it in new territories,' said Norva. 'Right, this yellow ribbon, let's have it.'

I looked up. 'There's the red flag.' I looked down at the map and pulled out the compass. 'And that way,' I pointed. 'Is North.'

'It is?' said Norva. 'I thought North was always, like, straight ahead.'

I shook my head. 'It's not.' I began walking in that direction, counting each step.

'There!' I pointed to a tree, its trunk wrapped in yellow ribbon. 'It was more than fifty steps, more like seventy-five, but we've done it.'

'Ayyy,' said Norva. She put her hands on her hips and turned around. 'But where to next then?' She put her hand to her forehead. 'It's getting a bit hilly,' she said, cautiously.

'Look at your feet,' I said. On the ground by the tree was a battered tin of biscuits.

'Oh, you want one?'

'No!' I said. 'I don't think there are biscuits in there –,'

She raised an eyebrow. 'Oooh, what do you think is in there, a toe, a finger – an eyeball?'

I winced. 'No. I'm hoping it's another clue.'

We surrounded the tin, looking down on its faded design.

'Go on, open it then,' Norva said.

'No,' I shook my head. 'It's definitely more of a Norva-based activity.'

'Totally is,' said Norva. She reached for the tin and forced its lid off.

14

I wasn't expecting a toe, not really, but I was surprised to see small-individually wrapped chocolate bars and cakes inside the tin.

'Is that it?' I said. I didn't mask my disappointment. I was invested now.

'I'd say it was a pretty good haul,' said Norva, between mouthfuls of Mars bar. 'I needed that.'

I stared at then shook the tin. 'But where's the next clue? It must be here.'

'Look everywhere,' said Norva. 'It has to be in the area.'

I turned the tin over, and there it was. The same handwriting, glued to the bottom of the biscuit barrel. Norva rested her chin on my shoulder as I read it aloud.

'Sweets for my sweet, sugar for the Stash. These next steps will take you closer to the cash. To get to the bottom, you must reach the top. Be mindful now, of that massive drop. Check your map; it's plain to see. Keep going, 100 m. NNE.'

I grabbed the map. 'OK, NNE means North-Northeast.'

'You're so smart,' said Norva, slightly awed. 'I would never have figured that out. I did get that we're going up a hill, though – that part was obvious. A bit overdone if you ask me.'

I brought the map closer to my face. 'Hmmm.'

'Hmmm what?'

'If we're going where I think we're going, then it is quite steep. It will be a serious climb.'

Norva looked behind her. 'Well, we've come this far, how bad can it be?'

Halfway up the hill, Norva leaned over and put her hands on her knees. She gulped down deep breaths of fresh air. 'Yeah, this is bad, really bad,' she said. 'I didn't know we had hills – no, this ain't a hill, no way, this is a mountain – like this in this country.'

I walked slowly to catch up with her and took in the view. Green as far as the eye can see. Sheaf Hill Hall, a small beige dot in the distance. 'It really is special, and I hate heights.' I smiled at my sister. 'I'll look forward to coming up here, once you've bought the Hall.'

Norva shook her head. 'The Hall can go to hell,' she panted.

'You don't mean that,' I said.

'I do. But imma keep going,' said Norva. 'I don't want the Hall – Thorney can keep it – but I do want the fame, and the fortune that's coming our way. How much further?'

'Just to the top there,' I pointed.

'But I can't even see the top,' she wailed. 'Why!?'

'It's just one foot in front of the other, stop being dramatic,' I said.

'We should have taken all of those Mars bars,' Norva said. We walked on.

As the sky came back into view at the top of the hill, voices rose from below it. Norva grabbed my arm. 'You hear that?' she whispered. I nodded.

'Help! Please, someone help us!' a voice called out.

Sophie's voice.

'It's the Harlows,' said Norva, shaking her head.

15

We peered over the edge of the hill. In the valley, about 30 meters below, Sophie lay in a heap, Tasha held her hand by her side.

'Hello?' Norva shouted down to them. 'You OK down there?' she said, knowing that they definitely were not.

Tasha let go of Sophie's hand and scrambled up the side of the hill, towards us. 'Nah! Don't leave me, Tash!' Sophie pleaded. 'I don't want to go out like this!'

'You ain't dying, Soph,' said Tasha. 'I'm getting help. It's why we were shouting, right?'

'Yeah, yeah. You're right,' Sophie whimpered. She squeezed her eyes tight and turned her head. 'My arm well hurts!' She held a yellow ribbon in her hand.

Tasha looked up at us. 'Can you get Ms Cocker or someone, please?'

I nodded. 'Yes, but what happened to you?'

'Yeah,' added Norva. 'How did you end up down there? I'm sure Ms Cocker didn't put this route on your map.'

Tasha narrowed her eyes. 'Well, how did you find us?'

I looked at Norva, she nodded. 'We heard crying, so we followed that sound.'

'We thought it was foxes at first,' Norva lied. 'We didn't want to see any animals hurt, so here we are.'

Tasha pursed her lips.

'You really need to tell us what happened,' I said. 'Because when we go back to the Hall, and tell Ms Cocker, we don't want to get you into more trouble.'

'You'll be in the deepest doo doo,' said Norva. 'That's for sure.'

Tasha sighed and swallowed. 'All right. Fine. This morning, Sophie found a note under our door –'

Norva reached for my hand and squeezed it tight.

'What did it say?'

'It had this little poem on it, telling us to follow yellow ribbons instead of orange flags.'

'We reckoned it had something to do with

that Sheaf Stash,' Sophie shouted up from below. 'We fancied a little adventure. A proper quest.'

'And you didn't write it yourself?' asked Norva leaning into the valley. 'You're creative, aren't you? Is this your…work?'

Tasha adjusted her balance and shook her head. 'No, she wouldn't. Sophie's a good writer – ask Paul Stanley – but she's not practical. Clambering up hills ain't her thing.'

'And it wasn't my handwriting, either!' Sophie shouted. 'I like cursive not capitals!'

'What time did you find this note?' I asked.

'Like after three? That's when I went to bed!'

'Three!?' said Norva. No wonder you slipped; you must be well tired.'

Tasha sighed. 'Nah, she's never tired, she's like my brother. This morning, when I woke up, about seven, we looked around to see who might have done this, who put this poem out.'

'And?' I asked.

'And,' said Tasha. 'Everyone was asleep, mostly. You two included.'

'Didn't I say stop spying on us?' said Norva.

I put my hand out to stop her. 'Carry on, Tasha,' I said.

'So, yeah, everyone was sleeping – apart from Ms Cocker and Millie. Ms Cocker's room was a state, and Millie, well, she must've gone out super early, because her bed was made and she wasn't in it.'

'Interesting…' said Norva.

'It is, isn't it?!' Sophie shouted.

'Do you have any more questions, Nik?' said Norva, biting the ends of her nails.

I shook my head. I looked down at Sophie who was trying to sit up. 'Are you two detectives or something?' she asked.

Norva looked at me and smiled.

'Something like that,' I said. 'Don't move, we're going to get help.'

16

Walking down the hill was a much speedier experience than walking up it. I had to curl my toes into my trainers to stop me from slipping down.

'The investigation begins!' said Norva leaping down the hill. She turned to look at me with a smile.

'It does, but we have to get help for those girls first,' I said.

'Nik, please,' said Norva, waving me away with her hand. 'We're queens of multitasking, this ain't no problem. Of course, we'll help them – they clearly don't have the range. Can you grab your phone? Can you walk and write?'

I nodded. I pulled it out of my pocket and opened the notes app. I didn't need signal for this. 'This… incident –'

'Which I'm calling it the Sheaf Stash Scam.'

'Fine. Someone deliberately – judging by both us and them receiving these clues – set a fake trail, which could have ended in serious tragedy. But who?'

'Not the Harlows,' said Norva. 'I thought they were shady, but like I said, they don't have the range.'

'They also wouldn't have deliberately hurt themselves and cry for help if that was the case. It's not them.'

'It has to be someone who works at Sheaf Hill Hall,' said Norva.

'Because they know these trails,' I added. 'But what about Ms Chan? She's lived around here, knows Ms Cocker very well, and said she wanted to win.'

'Good point,' said Norva. 'But Ms Chan, I just don't believe she would. She wants to win, sure, but then why would she send us into peril – peak peril? She wouldn't want us to die to win. Same goes for the teacher of the Harlows – if you really wanted to hurt your students, there's easier ways to do it. Closer to home.'

'Agreed,' I said typing into my phone. 'Then it's someone connected to the Hall. Let's take them in turn. Tom Thorne.'

'Thorney was the one who told everyone about the trail in the first place.'

'And we know he needs money for the Hall – he said that on the phone to his wife.'

'Would he put young girls in danger to do that, though?' asked Norva.

'He did call us poor girls – maybe he thinks we're disposable.'

Norva clenched her fist. 'He did, didn't he, that rat!'

'He was also having a happy conversation with Jake, the gardener, just before he left.'

Norva nodded. 'Tom's definitely a suspect.'

'What about Ms Cocker?' I asked.

'Something's going on with her and Thorney-boy,' said Norva. 'See the way they both looked at us as we started the trail?'

I nodded. I did.

'And she was with Ms Chan for most of the night, talking about the past – and Mr Thorne, and his wife. She's obsessed with him.'

'I don't know about that, Norva,' I drummed my phone against my lip. 'Tasha and Sophie said their clue came between three and seven thirty. We stopped eavesdropping at 12:45.'

'So, she had the time,' said Norva. 'And she wasn't in her bed early this morning, that's what the Harlows said. But… why would someone just mess up their own scheme like this? Their own business? It's not a good look.'

'Hmmm,' I wondered. 'It's really not. Unless.'

'Unless what?'

'Unless she was setting Tom Thorne up?' I offered. 'She did say it would be better for everyone if he left…or –' I thought quickly. '– maybe they're working together?'

'Ooh, I love both of those thoughts, look at that lateral thinking in action,' said Norva. 'Let's circle back on those later. Right, Millie, her assistant.'

'Well, Ms Cocker said she's very keen… maybe she set this up, so it would look bad, and she could run Girls Get Going! herself?'

'Solid theory,' said Norva. 'That works.'

'She was also up early –'

'Or she never went to bed,' Norva suggested. 'Ms Cocker did say she was very quiet. Perhaps she wasn't there at all. Maybe she –'

'Was with Jake Brook, the gardener?'

Norva nodded. 'Exactly. Him again. Creeping around in the early hours. Who knows what he was doing?'

'And with who.'

'Exactly, sis. Exactly,' said Norva.

Sheaf Hill Hall came into view. We I ran towards it. I gripped my phone, tightly.

Case: The Sheaf Stash Scam
Crime: Fake trail, ending in attempted murder, potentially.
Evidence: 2 x clues 1 - for us 1 - for the Harlows aka Tasha and Sophie.
Objects of interest:
*** Clues planted between 03:00 and 07:30.**
*** Yellow ribbon.**
*** Biscuit tin.**

Suspects ruled out: Tasha. Sophie. Their teacher Mrs Marsh. Ms Chan.

SUSPECT	JOB	MOTIVE	ALIBI	QUESTIONS
Mr Tom Thorne	Owner, Sheaf Hill Hall	To lose ownership of Sheaf Hill Hall? To get closer to Deborah Cocker?	Went home… but did he return to the Hall?	Did you return to Hall early this morning? What's your relationship with Deborah Cocker?
Ms Deborah Cocker	Director, Girls Get Going!	To frame Tom Thorne or working with Tom Thorne?	With Ms Chan, and then in bed, possibly?	Where were you between 03:00-07:30?

				What's your relationship with Tom Thorne?
Ms Millie Greenwood	Assistant, Girls Get Going!	Wants to take ownership of Girls Get Going!?	??? Location unknown. With Jake?	Where were you between 03:00-07:30?
Mr Jake Brook	Gardener, Sheaf Hill Hall	??? Assistant to Tom (and Deborah) or Millie?	??? Location unknown. With Millie?	Who are you working with? Tom or Millie?

17

Ms Chan, Ms Cocker and Millie were waiting for outside of Sheaf Hill Hall. We ran towards them.

'Wow! That was super speedy!' said Ms Cocker grinning at us. 'Finished already?'

'That's my girls!' said Ms Chan, beaming proudly. 'I *knew* you could do it.'

'Ah, but do you have the phrase?' said Ms Cocker.

'Yes,' I said between breaths. 'Owls or blades, lass? Owls or blades.'

Ms Cocker and Ms Chan looked at each other and squealed.

'That's it, that's the phrase, well done –'

'Thanks,' I said. 'But there's no time to congratulate us. There's a girl up there. She's hurt.'

'Possibly badly,' said Norva. 'A girl from Harlow. Sophie.'

The colour drained from Ms Cocker's already pale face. Ms Chan stared at us. 'What do you mean?'

'We mean someone went off their route, and now they're at a bottom of a big hill,' said Norva. 'Holding their arm, crying.'

'Oh my gosh!' said Millie. 'How did you find them?' Where?'

'We heard their cries for help,' I said. 'At the top of a big hill. North-northeast from here, I think.'

Norva shrugged. 'We couldn't just leave them, could we?'

'No, no,' said Ms Chan, worry etched on her face. 'You did the right thing. Well done.'

'Millie!' Ms Cocker shouted. 'Go grab the ropes and the first aid kit. Leave your notes and admin with Cindy.'

Millie nodded and thrust her clipboard at Ms. Chan. She ran into the hall and disappeared into the corridor.

Ms Cocker buried her face in her hands as she walked in circles. She rubbed her forehead. 'We do this activity *all* the time, why has it gone wrong today?' Her eyes welled with tears. 'I'm going to lose everything, Cinds. Everything I've worked for.' She stood still. 'It's him. *He* did this.'

Norva kicked my ankle.

Ms Chan put a comforting arm on her shoulder. 'You don't know that, and no, you won't. Like you say, you do this all the time, this was just an accident. It will be OK.'

'But what if it's not? What then? He's ruining my reputation!'

Millie reappeared with ropes and the first aid kit, and together they broke into a run, towards the trees. Ms Cocker turned back to face Ms Chan. 'You're in charge, just for a moment. Wait for the groups here, and, as they arrive, send them to The Gathering for a drink and a snack.'

Ms Cocker jogged back towards Ms Chan. 'And Cindy. Don't mention this to Tom, not yet. Please? I need to… get to him first.'

Norva and I held our breath as Ms Chan nodded. 'I won't,' she said. Ms Chan turned to us. 'You heard Ms Cocker. Go to the hall, grab a drink.' She bit her bottom lip and watched Millie and Ms Cocker run through the trees.

We walked into the entrance and Norva grabbed my arm.

'Don't worry, I'm not getting a drink,' I said in a low voice.

'Exactly. It's interrogation time,' she whispered. She wriggled her eyebrows. 'Starting with Tom.'

18

We stood in the doorway of Tom Thorne's office, as he squinted at his computer screen. He took his hand away from his mouse, sighed, sat back in his swivel chair and ran his fingers through his thick, black hair. He buried his face in his hands for a moment, and when he looked up, he noticed us looking. He sat up straight, then smiled.

'Alright there?' he asked. 'Can I help?' He looked at the heavy watch on his arm. 'It's almost 10:15, and you're back already? I haven't been here that long, but that's a record time for that trail, surely.' He smiled.

I didn't know what to make of him. Suddenly, he seemed… nice.

I looked at Norva and she stepped forward.

'Yeah, we do this kind of thing all the time,' she lied. 'It was easy peasy for us. Piece of cake.'

Tom sat back. 'Is that right? Then why are you here? On this scheme?'

Norva shrugged. 'Beats me, but I'm glad we are?'

'And why is that?'

'Because,' I spoke up. 'We can help you with your alternative trail, the Sheaf Stash.'

'We're really good at finding things out,' said Norva.

'And like you said, we're quick,' I added.

Tom laughed and waved his hand. 'You seem like smart girls.'

'You'd be right about that,' said Norva. 'Like Ms Cocker – she seems clever.'

Tom looked at Norva. 'Well, yes, she's a… good lass, old Deborah.' He coughed. 'So, I have to tell you, I *think* the trail's just a tall tale.'

'What?' said Norva. Her face fell, and her hands balled into tight fists. 'It's a scam?'

Tom nodded. 'I think so. Daddy used to love telling stories –always trying to find ways to make us go outside. I liked being indoors, mostly.' He looked out of the window. 'I was glad to go to boarding school to be honest. Away from here. Anyway, why? We're you thinking of giving it a go?'

'We… were, yes.' I said.

Tom shook his head. 'Wouldn't bother – plus it's not that safe if you don't know what you're doing.'

'Really,' said Norva, narrowing her eyes.

'Why mention it then? Why tell us at all?' I asked.

Tom sighed. 'That's what Deborah said, and it's a good point. I just... I just thought it would be fun, I suppose.'

'Or irresponsible. Either, or,' said Norva.

He stared at her, until the phone on his desk rang. 'Ah, that's Carla, my wife – she always calls around this time. He looked back at us. 'Well, it was nice to meet you. Enjoy your stay. What's left of it, anyway.'

19

Outside Tom's office, I opened my mouth to speak, but Norva put her finger to my lips.

'You don't have to keep doing that,' I said, brushing her away. You could just talk to me.'

'I know what you were going to say, though. You want to recap that conversation we just had with him,' she whispered.

I sighed and nodded. 'Yes.'

'See? I knew it, but I disagree. We don't know when Ms Cocker and Millie are going to get back – or when Ms Chan will be relieved of her duties, do we?'

I thought for a moment. 'So, we should we search their rooms? While we have the chance?'

'*Exactly*,' said Norva. 'We shouldn't waste it chatting, we can do that later.'

It made sense. 'Let's go. Ms Cocker's room first.'

We tried the door to Ms Cocker's room confidently, as we knew she wasn't there.

We hadn't bargained on it being locked, however.

I thought for a moment, drawing a map of the ground floor of the Hall in my mind.

'Her window faces the drive. We might be able to climb in –'

'Too risky,' said Norva, shaking her head. 'Everyone's walking in that direction, and Ms Chan is patrolling. Let's try Millie's and come back to Ms Cocker later.'

Fortunately, Millie's door was unlocked. Perhaps Norva was right, maybe she hadn't slept here at all. Just as Tasha and Sophie said, Millie's bed was made, her room was sparkling clean. Inside her room, I opened a wardrobe door. Empty.

Norva looked under her bed. 'Not a single suitcase, bag, pen – nothing.'

I sat on her bed and looked at the cabinet beside it. 'Wait, there is this.' I leaned over and picked up a framed photograph. I stared at the image. A small, curly haired girl stood in front of Sheaf Hill Hall, with an older man's arm around her shoulder.

'That definitely Millie,' said Norva over my shoulder. 'I'd recognise that hair anywhere.' She took the photo frame from my hand and stared at it. 'She was cute when she was younger. I wonder who the man is?'

'Same. Perhaps it's the owner of Sheaf Hill Hall? Tom's Dad?'

'Or maybe Millie's granddad or other relation?'

'Let's find out. It's odd, isn't it?' I said. 'That this photo is the only thing in her room?'

'It means it's very important,' said Norva. 'And if it's important, it's significant to our investigation. So, I'm just going to borrow it,' she put the frame into the pocket of her jacket. 'Just for a little while.'

'I don't like doing that, Norva. We have to remember to put it back,' I said.

'Put what back?' asked a voice behind us. I held my breath. I didn't want to turn around. 'What are you doing in here? Where is she?'

I looked over at Norva and she nodded. We turned around.

'I said what are you doing in here?' Jake Brook stood in front of us.

He held a bunch of wildflowers, tied with a yellow ribbon. The same ribbon on the vase in our room and on the tree trunks this morning. I looked at Norva and gestured towards it. She saw, she nodded.

'There's been some kind of emergency,' said Norva slowly.

'Emergency?' Jake replied. He blinked. 'What do you mean?'

'Yes,' I said. 'In the woods.'

'We don't know *exactly* what's happened,' said Norva. 'You know, teachers don't want to scare us.'

'We were asked to visit her room, to find her clipboard.'

'The emergency involves Millie?' Jake clutched the flowers to his chest.

I snuck a look at Norva. 'Yes,' she said, nodding gravely.

Jake took a deep breath and sat down on the bed. 'But that doesn't make sense!' he said.

'What doesn't?' I asked gently.

'Millie knows this place like the back of her hand, we grew up running around these hills.' He shook his head and gripped the bunch of flowers tightly. 'I told her not to do this. Not to take this *ridiculous* job. It's not like she needs the money anymore.'

I glanced at Norva. She stared back and shook her head.

20

Jake left his flowers for Millie on her bed. 'I'm going to find her and bring her home – it's the least I can do,' he said, striding out of her room. We followed behind him until he broke out into a run at the entrance of the Sheaf Hill Hall. We hung back outside The Gathering. I looked inside. Ms Chan was deep in conversation with teachers from other schools.

'So *that* was interesting,' said Norva, stroking her chin. 'Jake's *definitely* involved – maybe he did it? He has access to those ribbons.'

'And he was very concerned about Millie…he thinks *she's* hurt. If he set this fake trail, why? To make Millie would leave her job?'

Norva nodded. 'What he said about that was *very* interesting.'

'About her not needing money?' I asked.

Norva nodded. 'Yep. It was the *exact* opposite of what Ms Cocker said about Millie last night.'

'So, who's telling the truth? Ms Cocker or Jake?'

Norva shrugged. 'I'm just not sure yet, but I know the answer is in reach, I can just feel it in my stomach. Let's go look through Ms Cocker's window. See if we can glean anything from that.'

We quickly stepped past Tom's office, and ran outside, on the gravel then on the grass. I pointed to what I was sure was Ms Cocker's window. Norva stood shoulder to shoulder with me, and we looked in together.

Ms Cocker's room was messy, her bed unmade. Clothes in a heap on the duvet and on the floor.

'She's no Millie,' said Norva.

'No, she's not,' I said, 'But look there, in the bin, that's interesting.' Scrunched up yellow ribbon, on top of two wine bottles. 'It's the same ribbon we followed this morning, the same ribbon around Jake's flowers for Millie –'

'and the same ribbon around *our* flowers on the windowsill,' said Norva. 'We need to understand where it comes from – why do they have so much of it here?' She turned away from the window and put her back against the bricks.

I dug into my pocket for the note put under

our door this morning. Its uppercase letters, written in waterproof pen were a match for the alternative clues we followed on the trail earlier. I turned it over in my hand.

'This little crease at the top is interesting,' I said, showing it to Norva.

She peered at the paper. 'You sure that didn't happen in your pocket?'

I shook my head. 'No, that was –.'

'Oi, oi, wait, incoming,' Norva said, interrupting me. 'Look! The wanderers have returned.'

I looked in the direction of her gaze. Tasha, Sophie, Millie, and Ms Cocker were on their way back to the Hall. Sophie was limping slightly, and her arm in a sling. A sling made from Ms Cocker's North Face jacket. Sophie's face was tear-streaked, hair wind-swept, but she looked fine. I assumed she was because there were no ambulances.

There we no sirens to be heard. Just silence.

We walked towards the group, as Ms Chan exited the entrance of the Hall at the same time. Tasha, catching Norva and my eyes, nodded her thanks in our direction. Ms Chan leaned against the entrance, looking relieved for her friend.

On seeing Ms Chan, Ms Cocker dropped her shoulders and smiled. Millie, face contorted with concern, held Sophie's arm with one hand, and retrieved her clipboard from Ms Chan with the other.

The other girls, from other schools, began to gather on the grass – watching, wondering, whispering about this situation. They stared at the group as they walked into the Hall.

Norva and I followed behind.

21

When the group walked past Tom's office, he sprung from his seat and stood in his doorway.

He rubbed at his chin, then grabbed Ms Cocker's arm. Norva and I hung back to listen.

'What's happened?' he asked in a low voice. He looked up at Sophie, who was pouting and gulping at the air. 'I heard whispers of an accident. Everything alright? Do we need lawyers?'

Ms Cocker jerked her arm out of Tom's grip. 'How dare you?' she hissed. 'How could you?'

Tom took a step back. 'Deborah, what do you mean?'

Ms Cocker pointed at the Tasha and Sophie. '*These* girls were following yellow ribbons tied to tree trunks,' she spat. 'Sheaf Hill Hall gift shop ribbons! In search of the Sheaf Stash.'

'*What?*' Tom asked incredulously. 'That... that doesn't exist!'

'Oh, yes, Tom. It does now – in the imagination of all these girls,' Ms Cocker shook her head. 'Look, if you wanted to end our programme and kick Girls Get Going! out of the Hall, then you should've just talked to me, like an adult! Not set a trap! Not played one of your…games. I'm sick of this – sick of you!'

'But, but…I –' Tom began.

'*Do not* put my girls in danger!' Ms Cocker said, her eyes red.

'Deborah!' he pleaded. 'I would *never* do this – when would I have the time or the smarts to put something together like this?!'

Ms Cocker's chest rose and fell rapidly, and she breathed through her nose. She turned on her heels, in our direction. Norva and I quickly turned too, pretending to be interested in the map. 'Girls,' she said quietly. 'Go rest in your rooms, you've all had a tough morning. It will be lunch soon. Millie, go check on the status of the food.'

Millie nodded and ran into The Gathering. We followed Tasha and Sophie to their room. Norva and I stood at their doorway.

'You two alright then?' asked Norva. 'How bad is it?' she said, gesturing towards Sophie's arm.

'You know what, it ain't *that* bad,' said Sophie. 'I might be in shock, but I'm happy – I've got something to write about.'

'If you say so,' Tasha sighed. 'I was hoping to stay, get more sleep.'

Norva and I shared a confused look.

'Now we have to head back.'

'Why?' I asked.

Tasha jerked her thumb in Sophie's direction. 'There's not much she can do with a sprained elbow – that's what I think's happened. She's already called her dad to come get us. From his work, in London.' She closed her eyes and sighed. 'It is what it is, Tasha. Stress is no good for you.'

Sophie laughed. 'Exactly, Tasha, chill,' she said, rolling her eyes.

I looked around their room, spotting what I thought was their clue on a table pushed against the wall. I pointed to it. 'May I?'

Sophie nodded. 'But you can't keep it, OK? I'm taking that home.'

'Fine,' I said. I picked up their clue, and it was identical to ours, down to the strange crease at the top.' I nudged Norva to show her. 'See?' I ran my finger over the ripple. 'Exactly the same,'

I whispered. Norva nodded.

'What do you mean, *exactly the same*?' said Sophie, eyes narrowed. 'Wait. You *are* detectives, aren't you?'

'Yes,' I said. 'We are.'

Sophie smiled. Her eyes shone. 'I *knew* it,' she said. 'And I'm properly into it.'

The bell rang for lunch.

22

I was glad to hear that bell. I was hungry. Norva had a point; toast and jam was not enough food for the kind of morning we just had. We left Tasha and Sophie in their room, hoping to be first in the queue. We would eat, then immediately continue our investigation. I ran the suspects through in my head. I didn't think it was Ms Cocker anymore. She seemed very passionate when talking to Tom about her concerns with the Sheaf Stash. Tom. I was still unsure about him. He said he'd been to boarding school, doesn't like outside and spends most of his time her on the phone with his wife. Could he have set that trail? Really? He could have been working with Jake, however, – who I was certain was involved. Jake could have set the trap for Tom, to get him out of managing the Hall. Tom also could have set the trap to Millie, to force her to quit her this job, this job she didn't need.

Millie was waiting at the doorway of The

Gathering. She smiled when she saw us.

'I'm reyt chuffed to see you,' she said smiling. 'I wanted to thank you both for being *so* brave up the peaks this morning. If it wasn't for you – it could have been very sticky, very serious indeed.'

Norva shrugged. 'It's all right,' she said. 'We did what anyone else would have done.'

'I'm not so sure of that…' Millie said. She turned towards Tom's office, and then slowly back at us. She shook her head. 'Anyway,' she said, brightening. 'I've got a bit of admin for you if you don't mind?' She pulled a piece of paper from her clipboard and handed it to me. 'An incident report.'

'A report?' I asked. 'Because we discovered Tasha and Sophie?'

'Exactly,' said Millie. 'For health and safety. You know, a record, if we ever get investigated.'

'If?' Norva raised an eyebrow. 'More like when.'

Mille continued. 'But no rush on it. I'm due a little break now, so I'll come find you after lunch.' She patted me on the back, then walked in the direction of her room, down the corridor.

Norva joined the queue for lunch and stared at the offering. 'Chips,' she said. 'I'm going for that, bit a fish on the side? Yes! What about you?'

I hadn't looked. I was starting at the paper, instead. It was a basic report, with a table for us to fill in, describing what happened, when and to whom. The content of the page wasn't interesting, but the physical piece of paper was. At the very top of it, was a strange crease. I ran my finger along it, and my heartbeat sped up, rapidly.

'Norva…' I said.

'You're having chips, too? Knew it.'

'No, Norva, I think I've figured it out. The case.'

She turned to look at me, and I pulled on her arm, taking her out of the lunch queue.

'You better have,' she muttered. 'Soggy, cold chips suck.'

We walked to the furthest corner of the room, where we wouldn't be disturbed. I pulled the clue out of my pocket. 'Norva, I've been curious about this crease on our clue, and the one that also appears on the clue received by Tasha and Sophie,' I said.

She nodded. 'You have.'

'I wondered how it got there, where it might have come from.'

'Right…'

'We've just been given this report to fill in by Millie.' I handed it to her. 'Look at the top, just under the title.'

When she noticed, she gasped. 'Hand me the clue,' she said. I did. She lay the clue on top of the report. 'Oh my gosh,' she said. 'It's a dent from the clip on Millie's clipboard.' Her hand flew to her mouth. 'It's a perfect match!'

23

Lunch was now the furthest thing from our minds. Norva pulled Millie's photograph from her pocket as we strode through The Gathering, back to our room to discuss the evidence we'd gathered – to decide how we were going to formally accuse Ms Millie Greenwood – and Jake Brook of attempted murder.

Norva looked down at the photograph as she walked. 'Why, Millie? What was the *need* for this? What was the reason?'

I shook my head and stared at the image, too. 'To be determined, I have a theory that–'

My sentence came to an immediate stop when I bumped squarely into Tom Thorne, his car keys in hand. Our violent collision caused him to knock into Norva. She then dropped the frame, which smashed on the floor. We shared a guilty look, which Tom caught, before she dove on the floor to retrieve it.

'No, you don't!' said Tom, snatching the frame from Norva's hand. 'This is exactly why I don't want girls like *you*, here – taking things that don't belong to you.'

'We didn't take it!' said Norva.

'We kind of did,' I whispered.

'That's not helping, sis,' she said through tight teeth. Norva jumped to snatch the photo and its frame back from Tom's hands. He pulled it away and brought it close to his face.

'Wait a moment,' he said, standing still. 'Where did you get this?'

Norva shut her eyes and shook her head. 'Nope. Not telling.'

'What's Daddy doing with this little girl?' Tom rubbed his chin, while Norva pinched my arm. Tom turned the photo over and read the note on the back.

'Me and Daddy at my future house, September 1999.'

I stared at Norva. She was glaring at Tom. She jumped up and snatched the photo from his hands.

'To our room!' She said. 'Run!'

I did. It was a short run, only twenty meters or

so. When we got into our room, we threw our backs against the door, to bide some time.

'Oh my god, Millie and Tom are related,' Norva said breathlessly.

'And Tom doesn't know,' I said.

'Yet. But he's about to find out. He did say Daddy had other children, didn't he?'

I nodded. 'He won't believe they are so close to home.'

'Thieves!' Tom shouted from behind the door. 'Open up before I call the police!'

'Damn,' said a dejected Norva. 'We can't go out sad like this. Why do you think she did it? Quickly! Before we get arrested or worse – the cops take the credit!'

'Well, Jake said she grew up here, right?'

'Yep,'

'He also said she didn't need money anymore.'

'He did.'

'The back of the photograph said something about this being her future house?'

Norva turned it over. 'Yep, that's pretty much it.'

From outside our door, Millie shouted, 'Jake! Jake! Someone's been in my room!'

'The gang's all here,' said Norva. 'So, what's your verdict, Nik?'

I took a deep breath.

'Millie is Tom's sister. When their dad died, she got money, Tom got to run this place. But she doesn't want money. She wants the Hall. So, she's causing trouble.'

'She begged Ms Cocker for the job, to get back inside, to get closer,' added Norva. 'She's framing both her *and* Tom to get hold of the house. Two birds, one trouble treasure trail.' Norva shook her head. 'That's actually brilliant.'

Jake shouted in the corridor. 'There were two girls in here earlier, Mills. One with short hair, one with long plaits.'

'Busted,' said Norva. 'Busted by her accomplice.'

Ms Chan knocked on the door. 'Girls!' she hissed through the keyhole. 'What have you done?'

24

We stepped away from the door.

'Are you sure?' Norva whispered, holding the handle. 'You're ready for this?'

I nodded. It was time.

She pulled the door open. Outside, the corridor was crowded. Ms Chan was closest to the door, her arms folded across her chest. 'Explain yourselves,' she said through gritted teeth. 'And it better be good, because,' she jerked her head behind her. 'Everyone is here.'

She was right, everyone was. She was joined by Ms Cocker, Tom, Jake and Millie. Looking behind the adults, I could see Tasha and Sophie's door open, their faces peering out from the gap.

Norva took a deep breath. 'We've figured out what's happened,' she said. 'With the Sheaf Stash, the fake clues and the accident with the Harlows this morning.'

Ms Cocker stifled a light laugh. 'Girls. That's

very good of you to think you're helping, but… this isn't?'

'We received a clue last night,' I said. 'Exactly the same as Tasha's and Sophie.'

Ms Chan shook her head. 'A *clue?* And you never said anything?'

'Where's the fun in that?' asked Norva.

'We quickly determined it came from one of the adults here. Tasha and Sophie were also suspected, but quickly discounted.'

'Sick!' Sophie whispered from behind their door. Tasha nudged her silent.

'The clue came between 12:45 and 08:00 this morning, or so we thought.'

'Until we spoke to them two – they said they were asleep between three and seven thirty,' said Norva. 'So, it had to have been planted then.'

'At this point, we were excited by the clue, and decided to follow it, after we visited our first red flag,' I said.

'Wait a minute,' said Ms Cocker, putting up her hand. 'If you didn't go to all the flags, how did you figure out the phrase?'

'We overheard it last night,' said Norva. 'When you and Ms Chan we're giggling and gossiping.'

Ms Cocker looked at Ms Chan, who shook her head, but smiled.

'So, we followed these new clues, to find Tasha and Sophie at the bottom of the hill, crying it up.'

'We knew then they couldn't have been part of this plan. It had to be someone very familiar with the area,' I looked at Tom. 'We did think it was you, but you told us the trail was a tale and you didn't like being outdoors.'

'Yeah, you're right about that,' he said.

Norva turned to Ms Cocker. 'We actually thought you and Tom might have been in it together, but when we saw you light him up for putting everyone in danger, and how worried you were about you scheme. We knew it wasn't you either.'

Ms Cocker nodded. Her eyes wet. 'I would *never* hurt my girls or…*collude* with Tom. Never in a million years.'

'Say how you feel, Deborah,' Tom muttered under his breath.

We turned to Millie and Jake. 'So that left you two,' said Norva. They glanced at each other.

'This is ridiculous,' said Millie. She snorted. 'What, are we really going to listen to some little girls, about something so serious?'

'Exactly!' said Jake, emboldened by Millie. 'You want to hear what these... *thieves* have to say?'

Ms Cocker and Tom nodded. 'Yeah, we do,' he said. 'Carry on.'

'So, we saw Jake running round way after midnight,' said Norva. 'We knew you were involved, Jake – the yellow ribbon around the bunch of flowers you left for Millie matching the ribbons on the clues sealed the deal. But we didn't know *why*. Why you would do this. Or who you were working for.'

'And we were never quite sure about you, Millie,' I said. 'We heard that you were keen to take the job with Ms Cocker, but then you're very quiet. It was said that you needed this job, but you also didn't need money.'

'It made no sense,' said Norva. 'Until we put your clues together with the form you gave us.'

'What?' she said quietly.

'Look,' I said, aligning the clue with her health and safety sheet. 'The grooves on both documents match – and that groove came from your clipboard.'

'Let me see that!' said Ms Cocker, snatching the clipboard from Millie's clasp, and holding out her hand for our papers. 'They're... right,' she whispered. She turned to Millie. 'Why would you do this? I *trusted* you.'

'Because she wants Sheaf Hill House,' said Norva. 'And Tom? Meet your sister. That's baby Mills in the photograph.' Norva handed it back to Millie. 'Thanks for that,' she smiled. 'That was useful.'

25

'Absolute *brilliance*,' said Sophie from the next room. 'Tash, clap for me? My arm's still stinging.'

Tasha did. 'Seriously, that was wild! – Properly argued, well smart. I–'

Ms Cocker turned to the two of them. 'Thank you for your input, girls, but close the door? Let us deal with this.'

Tasha scowled and shut the door.

We all returned to looking at Millie, who was fidgeting with her fingers, looking down at her hands.

'Are you *really* my sister?' Tom said quietly.

Millie looked up at him and nodded. She sighed. 'Yes, yes I am.'

Ms Cocker and Ms Chan's mouths hung open. 'Never,' said Ms Chan.

'It's true,' said Millie. 'My mam used to work here, for most of her life. Turning the beds for the guests and maintaining it. And you know...

one thing led to another with our dad, and, well they had an affair. The result was me.'

Tom shook his head. '*Really?*'

'Really. He was always very kind to me, and he knew I loved this house. With my whole heart. He promised I could have it when he passed away.'

'But he left it to me,' Tom snorted. 'And I don't even want it.'

'He did leave me some money, and I will always be grateful, it's just that…' she looked up and to the ceiling, her eyes welled with tears. 'This house has so many memories for me. You were never around, Tom. You were older, at boarding school, then at university. It was me and Jake, all the time.'

'Jake?' said Tom, turning around to look at him. 'Your boyfriend, here?'

Millie shook her head. She put her hand on Jake's shoulder. 'No, not my boyfriend. My half-brother – our half-brother, Tom.'

'No. Way!' said Norva. 'Didn't see that coming. I had that all the way wrong.'

'We just want to return the Hall to its former glory,' said Jake. 'For us and for the locals who love it.'

'But you put *children* in danger to do so!' said Ms Chan. '*My girls!*'

'We did what we thought was best,' said Jake. He looked at Millie and sighed.

'I can't *believe* it was my clipboard,' Millie laughed bitterly. 'We'd planned it all so well, as well.'

"It was a great plan, Mills, putting all the yellow ribbon everywhere,' said Jake. He looked at Tom. 'Making you think I was working late on the gardens. All wasted.'

'I just had to get closer to my house, my Hall,' said Millie. 'Through Girls Get Going! or through you, Tom.'

'You know what you could've done?' said Tom, staring at her.

'What?' said Millie.

'Just told me the truth and asked me for ownership. I would have given it to you.' He rooted in his pocket for his phone. 'I'm calling the police,' he said. He stared at his screen. 'No signal.'

Norva sighed. 'Tell me about it, Tom,' she said. 'That's my biggest problem with your place, too.'

26

Pap was wrong and so was I. Leaving the city wasn't particularly *good* for us – not in a restful sense, anyway. It wasn't even a long weekend, in the end. It was just one day away. Once Tom called the police, and they took Jake and Millie with them, it was over.

No one wanted to sleep in Sheaf Hill Hall, no one trusted the activities, everyone wanted to go home.

Everyone apart from Norva.

She threw her bag into the minibus and sighed. 'It was *just* getting good!' she said. 'And, it's safe now– the troublemakers have gone, so what's the problem?'

'Get in the bus,' said Ms Chan.

'But I haven't even spent our fifty quid!' she wailed.

'In,' said Ms Chan.

I stared out of the window for most of the journey. Headlights and taillights blurred into bright balls of light as the sun went down. Norva sulked until her phone's signal grew in strength, and she was able to call George.

'Hey, Bestie!' She said, swivelling in her seat to get closer to the window. 'You will *never* believe what happened up here in the Peaks. We had a cosy, country case, you know?'

On the other end I could hear him shout, 'No way, give me all the deets!'

I closed my eyes for a moment, but Norva nudged me in the ribs and covered her phone. 'Did you see that? That sign just said London!' She snuggled down into her seat. 'I loved this journey for us.'

Happy
World Book Day!

As a charity, our mission is to encourage every child and young person to enjoy reading, and to have a book of their own.

Whether you enjoy **comics**, **fact books**, **adventure stories**, **recipes** – books are for everyone and every book counts.

On **World Book Day**, everyone comes together to have **FUN** reading. Talking about and sharing books with your friends and family makes reading even more memorable and magic.

World Book Day™ is a registered charity sponsored by National Book Tokens.

Illustration by Allen Fatimaharan © 2021

Where will your **reading journey** take you next?

1 Take a trip to your local bookshop

Brimming with brilliant books and helpful booksellers to share awesome reading recommendations, bookshops are magical places. You can even enjoy booky events and meet your favourite authors and illustrators!

Find your nearest bookseller at booksaremybag.com/Home

2 Join your local library

A world awaits you in your local library – that place where all the books you could ever want to read await. Even better, you can borrow them for **FREE**! Libraries can offer expert advice on what to read next, as well as free family reading events.

Find your local library at gov.uk/local-library-services

Scan here to visit our website!

3 Check out the World Book Day website

Looking for reading tips, advice and inspiration? There is so much to discover at worldbookday.com/getreading, packed with book recommendations, fun activities, audiobooks, and videos to enjoy on your own or as a family, as well as competitions and all the latest book news galore.

KNIGHTS OF is a multi award-winning inclusive publisher focused on bringing underrepresented voices to the forefront of commercial children's publishing. With a team led by women of colour, and an unwavering focus on their intended readership for each book, Knights Of works to engage with gatekeepers across the industry, including booksellers, teachers and librarians, and supports non-traditional community spaces with events, outreach, marketing and partnerships.